DOGGIE ANONYMOUS:
CANINE CONFESSIONS

What secret is your dog keeping from you?

By T.L. Champion

Doggie Anonymous: Canine Confessions © 2019 by T.L. Champion

Published and distributed on Amazon and IngramSpark. All rights reserved. No part of this book may be used or reproduced in any manner whosoever without written permission from the author except in the case of reprints in the context of reviews.

www.DoggieAnonymous.com

Library of Congress Registration Number: TXu 2-123-499
ISBN: 978-0-578-68792-6
Imprint: Independently published

DEDICATIONS

This book is dedicated to my older sister, Kim (human), and my little sister, Pandy (domesticated canine), who is now in doggie heaven.

Both have taught me the meaning of unconditional love.

WHAT IS DOGGIE ANONYMOUS?

We're a coalition of compulsive canines chronicling covert coping contingencies and conveying contemplative content throughout our community.

"Haley"
Director of the Doggie Anonymous Project

Since this is an anonymous canine confessional, just call me "Haley."

My sworn statement: I was directing a dog-umentary about the plight of the canine when I realized our message is bigger than a simple four-part series.

Therefore, I'm directing this behind-the-scenes pictorial, interviewing my comrades at Doggie Anonymous in hopes that it will benefit mankind.

And dogkind.

I hope it's a runaway best seller.

"Uncle Vinnie"
Executive Producer

Hey, what's-your-face. Yeah, you–holding 'dis book. Stop 'da laughing. We had a tight budget, okay? Dat's why we all sported 'da same shades.

I know what you're thinking: I'm the one who rocks 'em.

"Hank"
Cameraman

Here's an insider's exclusive: handle this information with a little T.L.C. and keep it on the doggie down-low.

Now be good.

Sit.

Stay.

Read.

"Preston"
President of Club DogAnon

You want to know why your dog does that crazy stuff. We're here to tell you. Consider the following the *Word of Dog*.

Here's what you don't know: Doggie Anonymous is a private society (yes, there's a secret paw shake), which gives us a safe space to air our grievances.

How do we do it? We meet at dog parks to discuss next steps. When you think we're sniffing each other's parts, we're actually exchanging classified intel. Other times we meet when you're at work. Sometimes we phone a friend. If you've been wondering why you burn through your "data" so quickly, well…

The following is a series of confessions from the members of Club DogAnon. **Names have been changed to protect the not-so-innocent. The sunglasses, leashes and disguises have come off. Consider this classified information to be shared on a need-to-know basis only.**

As President, I feel a sense of responsibility in letting "the establishment" know the plight of the canine. Therefore, I have green-lighted this dog-umentary and hired the best production crew to interview our members and uncover the truth:

What secret is your dog keeping from you?

RELEASE THE

HOUNDS!

"Ace"
Vice President of Club DogAnon

Welcome to Club DogAnon! Call me "Ace."

My canine confession: It was the Winter of 2015 and, oh my dog, it had been snowing for like a week straight. I still refer to it as "The Great Escape."

There was this pile of snow next to the fence and I just thought, "Dude, take your freedom back, *now!*"

So, I climbed it, jumped over and immediately felt this major *rush*. It was like this amazing, other-side-of-the-fence reality. It was otherworldly, man. The smells were intense. The possibilities, endless.

I howled, "Thank dog almighty, I'm free at last!"

Suddenly I heard the younger kid say, "Hey, there's a dog in the front yard that looks just like Ace. Wait! It is Ace!"

Twenty minutes later, after this intense, high-speed chase, they caught up with me and my emancipation was, like, over. W-h-a-t-e-v-e-r.

For the record: This is my doggie declaration: I'm planning my next vacation in Maui. Just try and stop me. I double dog dare you.

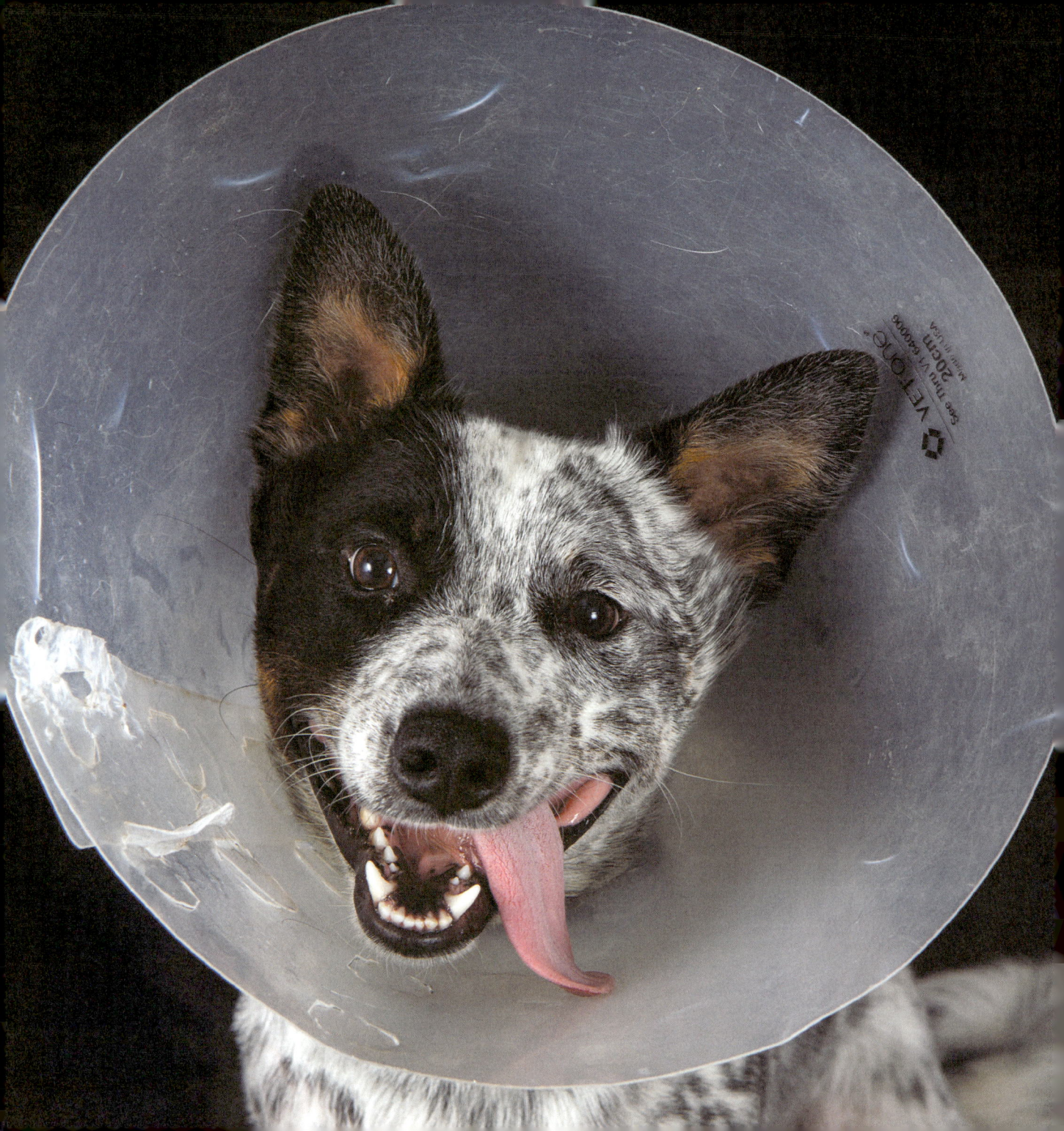

"Rufus"
Welcome Committee at Club DogAnon

My canine confession: It all started last Tuesday when the family left me alone. *So I blame them.*

As they locked the door behind them, I smelled something doggie delicious in the kitchen garbage can. Can you believe I was forced to jump over the baby gate to reach it?

I attacked it like a Pitbull on military detail and scored a bag of flour with chicken bits. Nice! But, as I enjoyed my hard-earned delicacy, my slobber mixed with the flour, forming a paste which stuck to my lips, tongue and nose. It dried instantly and *my jaw was floured shut!*

After the family returned, discovered my dilemma, howled with laughter and took pictures, they pried my lips open and cleaned my mouth with a little brush and some gooey stuff. Minty fresh, I must say. Num-num.

The tragic ending? Now they put this thing on me before leaving the house, even though I've announced I'm gluten free.

For the record: I don't want this incident to define me. And yet…

"Rocky"
Valet and Barking Lot Attendant

A confession from me? Fahgettaboudit.

Well... okay. Here's one for the record.

It's like 'dis: I wasn't so much eating Pop's paycheck as trying to collect my allowance 'ta buy him a gift.

The numbers on the bank draft—they weren't so tasty.

Father's Day is next week, see? But no matter how many times I 'splain it to him, he doesn't hear me. He's only worried about payin' 'da mortgage.

My intensions were good. I wanted to introduce him to a little culture with Muttley Crew's latest CD. Perhaps I ova-stepped my bounds. I see that now. In fact, Pops just applied for direct deposit and now my allowance has been completely shut off.

For the record: What can I say? There's more to life than having a roof over your head! Ahhh, fahgettaboudit.

"Missy"
Recent Doggie Day Care Graduate

Here's my confession: Sh-h-h. I hope Mommy isn't mad at me for changing my name for my confession. I love my Mommy. She really named me "Coco," after the exquisite designer, Coco Chanel. If the pearls fit, wear them, I often say.

Unfortunately, Mom's *insignificant* other thinks he's funny. He refers to me as "Coco Bean," "The Bean," and "Bean Dip With a Side of Guac."

I'm not a fan.

Yesterday I decided to show him how I feel about his behavior when I updated his Gucci jeans by chewing a "designer" hole in the crotch. Holes in jeans are "in" now, right?

Chanel would be so proud of this haute hound.

For the record: Later I gave his Air Jordan's a side of guac. Tee hee.

"Bennie" from the Bronx

You wanna confession? Here it is: humans aren't my favorite kind of people! We gotta show 'em who's running 'da show.

Take my people, for example. Last Halloween, they put 'dis prissy pink tutu on me, proceeded to point and laugh hysterically, and expected me to strut my stuff down Main Street.

Not on my watch.

So, I refused to move—even when they tried to pry me off the couch. Dead weight. I'm guessing that's the last time they'll spend $39.95 on a costume that hasn't been Bennie approved.

No fufu. And no tutu.

Who's in charge now?

For the record: Put 'da pumpkin outfit away unless you're gonna wear it.

"Lefty"
Self-Proclaimed "Opportunist"

My canine confession: I admit it. I overstepped my bounds when I "rescued" the pork chop from the Wilson's barbeque pit, but they *were* overcooking it. The way I see it, the real crime here is turning Grade A into common shoe leather.

They didn't need to call the authorities. To add insult to injury, I didn't realize I was being videotaped at the time of my transgression. I hope this means the footage is inadmissible, because I feel as if I've already been vilified in the court of public opinion, when, in essence, I simply "borrowed" the canine's equivalent of a cup of sugar.

For the record: My work is well done. I bring a lot to the table.

"Samantha"
Member at Club DogAnon

My canine confession: I'm a doggie darling.

Every Christmas, Santa puts something special under the tree just for me. He does this because I'm a good little doggie.

After everyone opens their gifts, Grandma comes over and we play a little game starring yours truly. First, the kids take my gift and kick it across the room.

Then they shout, "Get it, Sammy!"

So, I pounce on it and everyone watches. As I rip the paper with my teeth, I spit it out. Everyone laughs when they hear "Ptoui!" Then I unroll the paper to find the treat: a rawhide bone! Score!

Everyone applauds and I feast for the day.

For the record: I'm a living legend.

"Rustie"
Member of Club DogAnon

Call me "Rustie."

My canine confession: I wanna know what they do with "it."

Peoples are weird. In my family, I like the tall one best. He takes me for walks. Feeds me. Tells me his troubles. I like simple folk.

But I gotta tell ya, he follows me around the neighborhood with this plastic bag, collecting what he calls my "deposits."

I see other peoples following their doggies around with bags and I want to know what the heck they do with it once they get it? They must have it *stockpiled* somewhere by now. Right?

Is it a recycling project? A biology experiment? Or is it something more covert like Soviet missile testing using organic compounds?

For the record: What do they do with "it?"

"Floyd"
DogAnon Member

My canine confession: I NEED A DOGGIE DO-OVER!

It all started when this little kid was HOLDING A JELLY SANDWICH TOO CLOSE TO THE POOL!

He fell in. I jumped in the pool to **SAVE THE SANDWICH!**

Now everyone's upset that I didn't SAVE THE KID.

Yes, he's fine. The water wings helped.

What people don't understand is I averted a double disaster, which would have been letting the soggy sandwich go to waste.

For the record: Son of a pup! IT'S NOT MY FAULT TIMMY'S A CLUTZ!

"Madelaine"
Membership Committee at Club DogAnon

Here's a bit of advice: if you want people to like you, *be adorably cute*. Or get an adorable pup because we make you look good.

If you're looking for a hook-up, a beautiful doggie can help you attract Ms. Sweetheart or Mr. Sensitive. Of course, daily walks in the park are also a critical element.

For example, my doggie demands are quite simple: I need monthly grooming, two squares a day, an assortment of treats, and remember, I tend to look even *more adorable* when my *new* chew toys are easily within reach.

For the record: I'd love to stay and chat, but I'm late for my mani-pedi. Just look at these cuticles!

"Farnsworth"
Ditch Digger

My canine confession: I take issue with the fact that I don't get to go on daily bye-bye rides with the rest of the family. *They know how much I love feeling the wind in my fur and the sun on my muzzle!*

Yesterday I got so angry that I took it out on the couch cushions. Note to self: they really don't taste as good as you'd think.

This morning, I realized I need to stop this compulsive behavior, forgive, forget and hit the reset button. So, I went outside and buried the past, next to the steak bones, in the Johnson's backyard.

For the record: I'm deconstructing the ugliness to find the beauty within.

"Milo"
Secretary at Club DogAnon

Here's my confession: So, 'da cat.

Let me ask you 'dis: would you like it if someone was always pawing at you? Waking you up? Stealing your food?

And what's worse? My family rewards him for 'dis behavior because "he's so cute."

Hate. Him.

What Mr. Snickers—and the rest of the family—doesn't know is, he's living on borrowed time. And when I snap, I can't be held responsible for my actions because we're talking about years of abuse. In dog time, 14 to be exact.

I'm taking notes, documenting his behavior and planning his *exit* strategy. It's about to get real in here.

For the record: Sweet mother of dog, Mr. Snickers is going down and it ain't gonna be pretty...

"Debbie"
President of "Every Dachshund Has Its Day"

My canine confession: My brother, Beauregard Bull Boxer, is my best friend. He considers himself a professional frolicker. Especially when it comes to freshly fallen snow.

If the powder is up to his eyeballs, he doesn't care. He'll show off his mad skills, pouncing in the drifts and catching snowflakes in his mouth, making everyone laugh.

That Beau is a clown.

Okay, I admit it. I'm jealous. I wish my short, stubby legs were made for speed. Or height. Or distance.

In the winter, they send Beau out first, and he does his doggie due diligence by carving out a path–especially for me–in the drifts of snow. Then I can do my doggie thing, while cautiously watching for avalanches.

For the record: Dog bless you, Beauregard Bull Boxer. You're my hero.

"Beau Bull Boxer"
Professional Frolicker

My canine confession? What? You want me to spill my guts?

Okay, *I did it.*

Last Thursday, I was so glad when Mom came home from work. I was doing my doggie happy dance when she saw the mess in the kitchen. Of course, I tried to tell her that she just missed the burglars who ate her meatloaf.

When she asked me who did it, I gave her a description: tall, furry and good looking. With the face of a Greek dog.

She responded by saying, "And the culprit still has gravy all over his mouth! Bad boy! That was supposed to be my dinner!"

Psst. Can you tell her I get a little hungry and bored when she's at work all day?

For the record: I take the blame, just not the responsibility.

"Max"
Ambitious Over-Retriever

Call me "Max."

My canine confession: I consider myself an ambitious over-retriever. My human brother, Frankie, loves to throw things to see what I will bring back. So far, I haven't let him down. Balls, frisbees, sticks and rocks.

Sometimes I go rogue. Once I did a doggie dash through the neighborhood, then brought back a license plate. You should have seen the look on his face! Like I ate the car it was attached to or something!

Ha!

What Frankie doesn't know is—I do things just to make him laugh. His laughter is the best sound in the world. I've even invented a game to see how many tennis balls I can fit into my mouth at once.

For the record: My family claims that my grasp on reality is a little far-fetched.

"Angel"
Fitness Instructor

My canine confession: My humans would never get away from the computer if I, like, didn't make them take me out regularly.

Seriously, I mean, I've improved the quality of their lives with exercise and fresh air. They're so lucky to have me.

In fact, I've noticed a direct correlation between their elevated happiness levels and my receipt of new chew toys.

My work here has been totally transformative.

For the record: I'm the doggie darling of daily decompression.

"Russie"
Food Sampler

I'm not sure this is a confession, but... I think Mommy's mad at me.

I really didn't mean to eat the whole apple pie (burp). It started as a nibble. But then it occurred to me: did she really put what smelled like hot deliciousness on the table to cool–or is she looking for my professional opinion?

Everyone knows I can't resist a crumb topping!

I just don't get any appreciation for the sacrifices I make around here. I mean, that pie was *hot!* And yet I kept going, willing to take one for the team.

But all I heard was, "Bad dog! Bad dog!"

Would a simple "thank you" now and then be too much to ask?

For the record: Next time bake *two* pies. One within reach and one for "company." Whoever that is.

"Vinnie"
Inspector at Club DogAnon

My canine confession: For dog's sake, I was chasin' Howard 'da squirrel 'cuz he owes me a fiver from the track last week. He wanted to pay me in nuts and I told him steak bones are my only form of currency.

Everyone knows 'dat.

I can't be seen as "soft" or 'da pack will turn on me.

For the record: Truth be told, I would have accepted kibble. But for 'da love of dog, Howard, just stick to 'da script.

"Trixie"
Expert on Human Behavior

My canine confession: You want to know what I think of people? That's classified. But, if I can speak off the record, I will tell you that as a specialist in the field of psychology, I've learned that humans are *not* a highly sophisticated breed.

Eat. Sleep. Go outside. That's what their lives consist of.

Although, in their defense, they make great companions, love to cuddle and retrieve Frisbees at an impressive pace.

For the record: Dog bless them, after all, they're *only* human.

"Hank"
Fellowship Coordinator at Club DogAnon

My canine confession: I have a doggie dilemma. My family is THE MOST IMPORTANT thing in the world to me, but apparently the devotion doesn't cut both ways.

Case in point, yesterday they went to the beach—without me. How do I know? Because I smelled the sand in their shoes and the barbeque on their breath. Smokey Mesquite! They were probably laughing behind my back the whole time...

Of course I was TICKED! But no one seems to care about my little *unimportant* feelings...

Don't worry, dear family. I'll just be laying here.

All day long.

Waiting for you.

For the record: Can I go if I promise to be a good boy?

"Blue"
Internal Affairs at Club DogAnon

My canine confession: I can't speak for all four-leggeds, but when it comes to love, canines can fall hard. And they love deeply.

In fact, I'm having a difficult week because Crystal, the Schnauzer down the street, refuses to return my calls. She left me for a Shepherd named Bruiser, even though everyone knows he's all brawn and no brains.

Since the breakup I can't eat. Can't sleep. The only thing I want to do is play dead.

For the record: She was my one and only. Dog. Gone.

"Rex"
Relationship Manager at Club DogAnon

Call me "Rex."

My canine confession: From exhaustive field research, my study of humans has brought me to one inescapable conclusion: people seek love and affection as much as—if not more than—food and shelter.

The females are my personal area of study: they are generous with the belly rubs, love taking naps and prefer long walks on the beach. I've also discovered they are pushovers for soulful eyes and a hairy chest.

Do you hear that, Clooney? Kiss my scooper!

For the record: I'm dog's gift to women.

"Heidi"
Food Critic in Training

My canine confession: I don't know why I do it. I blame the call of the wild. It kinda takes over and I even feel a little "wolfie" at times. It's like my ancestors are *making me* root through yesterday's garbage with a frenzy I can't control. It's really not my fault.

Plus, everyone knows day-old pizza is still good.

And the delicious-chocolate-cupcake-with-sprinkles incident wasn't my fault either. You never should have left them on the coffee table, assuming they were out of reach. My natural killer instinct just kicked in and…a sacrifice had to be made.

For the record: I'm too cute to be held accountable.

"Buster"
Unemployed Motivational Speaker

Here's a confession: The holidays are approaching and, for the record, I want everyone to know that I HATE SANTA!

He's LAME!

Last year's holidays were a TOTAL BUST! Claus overlooked my annual rawhide AND I was TOTALLY FORGOTTEN BY MY OWN FAMILY! In the rush of the day they forgot to FEED ME! No kibbles. No chew toys. No nothin'.

MERRY CHRISTMAS, BUSTER!

And I was a GOOD BOY all year…well, um, unless you count the incident with the Lipchitz's shiatsu, Trixie. Hey, how was I s'posed to know she was talking about her new choke collar when she used the words "doggie style."

I bet Santa is picking out her new leash now.

For the record: This year I'm giving Claus the doggie deep freeze.

"Spike"
Dog School Drop Out

Declaration: For dog's sake, why am I not considered a priority in my own home? How many times do I have to whine about this?

Yes, I kicked my dish across the floor last night! Doesn't my family realize my needs must be taken seriously?

As a beloved member of this household, I believe I've earned a place at the family dinner table.

Ask yourself this: do you want to eat canned crap in a bowl off the floor?

For the record: My list of doggie demands will be complete by sundown. This is no longer up for debate.

"PAWlene"
Dogtorial candidate and member of Club DogAnon

My canine confession: My humans sent me to doggie day school to correct "behavioral issues." What no one expected was my passion for higher learning.

I earned my Bachelor of Arfs degree and now I'm a highly sought-after speaker.

Woof!

As the pack leader in my family's household, I plan to earn my master's degree before my master does.

For the record: Hot diggety dog, I excel at everything I do!

"Sadie"
Treasurer at Club DogAnon

My canine confession: Sweet mother of dog! I'm embarrassed, but it's true. People are afraid to get near me when I'm eating because I gulp down my food and growl if anyone comes near my bowl.

At first, I denied these accusations, but now I'm digesting the truth. I believe my eating disorder stems from psychological episodes due to "Large Litter Syndrome."

Being the runt of the litter came with certain challenges, but I realize my past doesn't have to define my future.

For the record: I'm working on my doggie decorum.

"Carruthers"
Self-Proclaimed Mamma's Boy

My canine confession: The storm last night was LOUD! Ka-boom!

Mom noticed I was scared and shaking! So, she came down to the floor and slept next to me. *We snuggled tight!*

This morning she woke up with a sore back. Ouch. Poor Mom.

But I have an idea and I can't wait to tell her! Wouldn't it be easier on her next time if I just climb *up on the bed? I would do that for her!*

I know I'm not allowed up there—*when she's home*—but it would be so much easier on her the next time we have thunder booms. I promise not to take up the whole bed.

For the record: I love you, Mom, and I'm only looking out for your well-being!

"Sweetie Pie"
Joyride Enthusiast

My canine confession: Yesterday, I went for a bye-bye ride with my humans. Even though I yelled "shotgun!" they pretended not to notice.

"Honest to dog," I demanded, "I'm TIRED of taking the back seat in life!"

But did they care? No! They just turned up the radio, ignoring me completely!

So, I thought, "I'll show them!" That's when I stuck my head out of the window, giving them the silent treatment!

Next time I'm going to demand that they let me drive. After all, how hard can it be? You just keep it between the lines, right?

For the record: I'm a defiant doggie. It's how I roll.

"Zeus"
DogAnon Welcome Committee

Call me "Zeus."

My canine confession: Contrary to what Elmer said, I wasn't biting him so much as personally welcoming the hem of his khaki jacket into our living room. New neighbors can be a little shy at first, so after answering the door, I considered shaking his hand, but it was in his pocket.

So, I gently pulled him into the house—and we immediately started playing the tug-of-war game. I thought, "What a great neighbor!"

My parents seemed to be shocked at my social skills. Then they played the game of putting me in the laundry room.

Later, Mommy and Daddy scolded me saying that Elmer will never visit again because of what I did.

For the record: Someone please send him my apologies. Remember, Elmer: to err is human, to forgive—doggie divine.

"Digger"
Neighborhood Watch

My canine confession: As head of the Neighborhood Watch Committee, I must admit, my last mission was grueling. Most people don't realize the type of high-level security involved in my line of work.

After careful evaluation, I surveyed the area and made "the drop" on the perimeter of the Miller's tree lawn.

For the record: Please don't blow my cover. I'm a professional with a license and everything. Wait, I'll get my tags…

"PETunia"
Landscaper

My canine confession: Okay, I admit it, I'm a perfectionist.

Everyone knows the yard is *my* territory and they missed a spot when they mowed it yesterday. I've complained in the past, but they've always ignored me.

So, I chewed the grass down evenly, then presented it to them on the living room rug to make my point heard!

For the record: You *must listen* to the still, small woof of dog.

"Homer"
Member of Club DogAnon

Grievance: Call me "Homer." Puppy professionals have categorized my depression as stemming from "Premature Separation Anxiety," based on the fact that I was kicked out of the litter too early.

This has manifested itself in two ways. First, because I have an intense desire to find love from everyone I meet, even strangers, I give kisses freely, licking people's faces in an effort to gain their approval.

Apparently, some people don't like that...

Second, I've been accused of "sleeping around," mostly from the chair to the bed to the ottoman.

I'm. So. Tired.

For the record: I don't care what they say, I'm not a promiscuous pup.

"Schultzie"
Retired Marine

My canine confession: Hey, 'da reason I howl at 'da moon is to let everyone know I'M NOT HAPPY.

First, my love life's a mess since 'da Labra-doodle moved in next door. I can't concentrate! I keep seeing her through 'da fence. I'm entranced by her: she looks right into my soul!

Bow. WOW!

In addition, my job as head of security is in question since they installed 'da new alarm system. Don't they know I need 'dis job and the bennies, including my 401 rollover?

True dat.

For the record: I'm willing to work at my day rate. Plus expenses.

"Bailey"
The Bandit

My canine confession? I gotta funny tail for ya. My owners don't know it, but I help myself to some daily doggie deliciousness without them ever knowin'!

It's a covert operation.

'Ya know how sometimes 'ya just get a hankering for a little sumpthin' sumpthin'? Me too!

Yesterday, for example, it was spaghetti–right from the little one's plate! Delish!

No one was hurt and no was the wiser. Sh-h-h.

Last week it was a piece of Halloween candy, although later someone had to clean up the backlash from that one. My apologies to the living room rug. And the ottoman. What can I say? I have a delicate constitution.

Later this afternoon, I'm plannin' the "birthday cake heist extravaganza" starring Bailey, the Bandit. Hey, I love Mom's buttercream frosting!

For the record: I'm a doggie daredevil.

"General"
Retired Special Ops

You want me to confess my "sins?" Unreal.

Let's just say that after years of service in the military, I believe I've earned the right for a little fun now and then. Let me state for the record that skinny dipping in the Malinowski's pool while they're on vacation is not a federal offense! It's a form of doggie nirvana.

Curses on the Puparazzi!

For the record: Dog only knows, what I do on my time is my business!

"Pandora Pooh"
Sculptor

My canine confession: My name is Pandora, but my family calls me "Pandy-Pooh." I know it's because I look like a cuddle-bear, but they cite another reason.

I don't care what they say, I'm not in the business of "manufacturing."

In fact, I consider myself an artist, creating my body of work, "When Nature Calls," on a daily basis for my followers.

My next showing is planned for the Johnson's tree lawn, next to the hydrangeas.

For the record: As an artist, I specialize in post-consumer waste, creating regular content for my blog.

"Pavlov"
Member of Club DogAnon

You want my confession? Here it is: I blame my humans for my problems.

There. I said it.

Case in point: did you know that because of my parent's barbaric decision to paper-train me as a pup, I can no longer look at the "business" section of the *Times* without gut-wrenching flashbacks?

For dog's sake, it's like canine Turbo-Laxx!

As a result, I'm permanently banned from doggie day care!

For the record: From now on, I'm putting my trust in dog.

"Lady"
Relationship Expert

My confession: I'll admit, it was an elaborate scheme devised by the canine population centuries ago, but as the legend goes, once we became organized, it was easy.

It all started when we became the humans' hunting companions… but soon it was so much more.

Over time, we slowly moved into their space offering them something they often can't get from their own kind: unconditional love.

For the record: We truly are a national treasure.

"Preston"
President of Club DogAnon

In closing, I'd like to thank you for your time.

As champions of the canine cause, we're spreading the word of dog: canines are emotional, intelligent creatures! Just like humans, we all want to live happy, fulfilled lives.

Thanks to all who have opened their hearts–and homes–to us. Your love and kindness have not gone unnoticed.

You are truly making *man*–dog's best friend. Dog bless you.

"Haley"
Director of the Doggie Anonymous Project

That's our tail.

We hope you enjoyed these canine confessions. Thank you for helping us celebrate the irresistible weirdness of dog.

Cut!

That's a wrap!

MAY DOG BE

WITH YOU.

About the Author (and her dog)

T.L. Champion likes to give a voice to those who can't speak for themselves. An award-winning writer, professional writing coach and creator of the *Become a Published Author System*, T.L. lives in Cleveland, OH, and surrounds herself with real and fictitious friends and family.

As a child, T.L. was introduced to a Lab-Springer puppy that immediately bit her on the face. That puppy later became her best friend. Growing up in a dysfunctional home as many of us do, T.L. convinced herself that her new dog, "Pandy," was indeed her little sister, thereby increasing her "sphere of love" within the family unit.

Young T.L. believed that Pandy saved her life with a simple mix of love and companionship. Whether it was time for another doggie dress-up, tug-of-war or secrets to be shared, the duo delighted themselves with hours of fun and mischief.

T.L. Champion is available for speaking opportunities as she plans her DogAnon world tour. If you'd like to book an event, contact her at **TL@Champion-Studios.com**. More information can be found at DoggieAnonymous.com.

About the Photographer

Maria Sabala, canine's best friend, received enough slobbery kisses to last a lifetime during the Doggie Anonymous audition where she worked with the silly, well-trained, actor/models for this book. In fact, she has described the three-day event as one of the best experiences she's had as a photographer. Maria takes pet portraits (and lives) in Cleveland, OH.

As a child, Maria grew up with Misty and Maggie, who proved to be the cutest Beagles–but the worst sled dogs. In 2008, she started her own photography business, Maria Sabala Photography, when her first-born son was five months old.

Naturally, she was drawn to photographing babies, but over time, she started capturing shots of the canine population, wondering how she could create a collection to showcase her work. She's finally able to do that in *Doggie Anonymous: Canine Confessions*.

As a pet photographer, Maria offers beautiful portraits of pets that range from the typical 8 x 10 photo to beautiful, oversized canvases to hang over the fireplace. (With Fido's approval, of course.)

ACKNOWLEDGEMENTS

To our sponsors, partners and favorite organizations:

A special thank you goes to Sit Means Sit! This dog training facility in Avon, Ohio, helped us recruit the handsome pooches included here. Without them, we wouldn't have been able to stage the photoshoot that inspired this book—and the "cute" factor would have been seriously compromised.

Thank you to Michael Homan, Corey Homan and Leslie Richards. Our gratitude and love also goes to Kyle Lemmer who lost his dog Raiden (the black & white cattle dog wearing the cone in this book).

A Big Thank You Goes to the Following!

Friends, Family and Colleagues: Lisa Marie Brusso, Kim Champion, Maria Jeancola, Rick and Mark Phelps, Karen Curtis, Mary Lee and Vernon Altman, Shana Mysko, Maia Beatty, Jim Pelyhes, Amy Westover, Mike Chisler, Kathy DeLong, Chris and John Krasnobrucky, and Andre Calilhanna.

Doggie Models/Actors and Their Parents: Manny and Shana Mysko; Oliver, Tracy and Lynn Walker; Lucy and Kristi Slabe; Cooper and Victoria Weatherwax; Dewey and Nate Courtney; Daisy, Anthony and Heather Costanzo; Calypso, Pandora and Oksana Savinell; Kloe and Leslie Richards; Marco and Mindy Nielsen; Schnitzel and Danielle Campbell; Ziggy and Susan Bishop; Charlie and Jennifer Tulli; Nakia and Lindsay Bedient; Earl, Pepe and Jean Sikora; Peanut, Radish and Brad Roller; Sproket and Diane Graham; Penny Lane and Leslie Bryant; Cooper and Marcia Markey; Samantha and Charles Russo; Gracie and Joyce Klotzbach; Teddy and Kris Hoover; Dixie and Jill Petitti; Olive and Lindsay Haywood; Callie, Raiden and Kyle Lemmer; Malty and Felix Markowski; Petey Pie, Louise and Julie Moffitt; Lulu and Joan Barrus; Sheldon and Alison Lemmer; Dexter and Erica Verheyen; Riley, Diesel, Moe, Brian and Lauren McCall; Thumper, June Bug and Elizabeth Rogers; Rocket and Corey Homan; Romo and Lindsey Homan; Tana and Anne Cornelius; Triton and Brittany Alemane; Enzo and Ryan Schickenvantz.

A Note from the Author of Doggie Anonymous: Canine Confessions

This book has been a labor of love for me. As mentioned, I feel like my dog, Pandy, saved my life as a child. As many of us have experienced, I grew up in a dysfunctional family, but Pandy always provided me with the kind of love and companionship that children crave.

I also wrote this book for these reasons:

1. The world seems to be a very serious place right now. One of my goals in creating these stories was to inject a little humor and lightness into the atmosphere. I hope I've accomplished that goal.

2. It's important for me to promote organizations that help our furry-faced, four-legged friends (and family members). Therefore, we are partnering with several facilities that support canine causes.

3. I wanted to promote a local (CLE) artist and when I met Maria Sabala, I knew I'd found the right partner for my project! Her portraits are beautiful!

4. As a professional writing coach, I meet a lot of writers who are upset with themselves because they are not starting, finishing or publishing their books. I hope to inspire these authors by showing them that not all books need to be lengthy, 200-page novels or derived with Shakespearean-like content. Let's find something we're passionate about, write a story, and share it with the world!

We Want to Reach a Wider Audience. Will You Help?

If you believe this book is worth sharing with friends and family, I'd be honored if you'd take a few seconds to share your thoughts on FaceBook, Instagram or your favorite social media platform. If it makes a difference in their lives, they'll be forever grateful. So will I.

T.L. Champion, author of Doggie Anonymous: Canine Confessions.

For coaching opportunities related to the Become a Published Author System, go to **Legacy-Coach.com** or contact me directly at **TL@Champion-Studios.com**.

Follow us on Instagram at ClubDogAnon or visit **DoggieAnonymous.com**.

Lightning Source UK Ltd.
Milton Keynes UK
UKRC021504021220
374405UK00010B/272